BeiHmnr

EGMONT

We bring stories to life

This edition published in Great Britain 2010 by Dean,
an imprint of Egmont UK Limited
239 Kensington High Street, London W8 6SA

Thomas the Tank Engine & Friends™

CREATED BY BRITT ALLCROFT

Based on The Railway Series by The Reverend W Awdry
© 2010 Gullane (Thomas) LLC. A HiT Entertainment company.

Thomas the Tank Engine & Friends and Thomas & Friends are trademarks of Gullane (Thomas) Limited.
Thomas the Tank Engine & Friends and Design is Reg. U.S. Pat. & Tm. Off

HiT entertainment

ISBN 978 0 6035 6522 9
1 3 5 7 9 10 8 6 4 2
Printed and bound in Italy

Thomas, Percy and the Funfair

It was the day of The Fat Controller's funfair. There would be fireworks and fairground rides for all the children.

There was to be a special visit
from the Chinese Dragon too.
Percy was delighted. He thought
the Chinese Dragon was the most
exciting thing of all.

The Fat Controller arrived at
Tidmouth Sheds. He had come
to give the engines their jobs.

"Edward," he said. "You will pull
the merry-go-round. Henry, you
will pull the roller-coaster.

Gordon will take the fairground people and Toby, the bumper cars. James and Emily will take the Ferris Wheel. And Thomas," he boomed. "You are to collect the fireworks and the Chinese Dragon."

"What's my job, Sir?" asked Percy, hopefully.

"You are to collect the coal from the Coal Plant and take it to all the stations," ordered The Fat Controller. "A railway can't run without coal. It's a very important job."

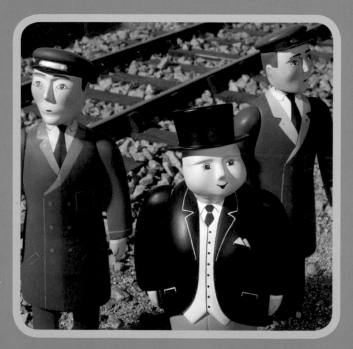

All the engines were very excited
... all except Percy. He felt very
left out.

Percy chuffed sadly over to the Coal Plant. This didn't feel like a very important job at all.

When he arrived, there was a long line of trucks. "I wish I was pulling

something exciting," he grumbled. "Not boring old trucks!"

So, he left the trucks and pulled out of the Coal Plant.

Along the line, Percy met Toby.
He puffed past, happily pulling
brightly coloured bumper cars.
The children in a nearby school
clapped and cheered.

Then, Edward chuffed past with
the merry-go-round. The children
cheered even louder.

Percy thought that Toby and
Edward were having a wonderful
time doing their jobs.

Suddenly, Percy had an idea!

"Maybe Edward and Toby need some help? Helping friends is much more important than delivering coal!" he wheeshed.

Percy forgot all about his job collecting the trucks at the Coal Plant. He steamed away after his friends instead.

Toby and Edward had stopped
at a red signal.

"Do you need any help?"
Percy peeped.

"No, thank you, Percy," said Toby.

"We can do it!" chuffed Edward.

Percy was sad. He wanted to do
something for the funfair too.

Then, Percy saw James and Emily
at a Crossing. They were pulling
the Ferris Wheel.

"That looks like fun!" thought Percy.
"I'm sure they'll need some help."

But James and Emily didn't need
any help either.

Then, Percy saw Gordon waiting
at a signal.

Gordon was pulling the fairground
people. But he didn't need any help.

"Goodbye, little Percy," he said,
and wheeshed away.

Then, Percy saw Henry on
the bridge. He was pulling the
roller-coaster.

"That must be really exciting,"
peeped Percy. "I am sure Henry
would like some help."

But Henry didn't need any
help either.

Percy chuffed away slowly.
He was feeling really glum now.

He found Thomas waiting at
the next signal. Thomas was
carrying the fireworks and the
Chinese Dragon.

"That looks like the most fun of all!" gasped Percy.

But Thomas didn't need any help pulling the Chinese Dragon and whooshed straight past Percy.

Percy had forgotten all about his
important job.

And now, there was trouble . . .

James was stuck on the line.
"There's no coal at the stations!"
he called to Percy. "We've all
run out!"

"Oh, no!" cried Percy. "If the engines don't get some coal, the funfair won't open. And it will be all my fault!"

Percy knew what he had to do.
He had to pick up his trucks and
take the coal to the stations as
quickly as he could.

Percy wheeshed all over the Island,
delivering coal to his friends. Now,
he was really able to help them.

Soon, everyone's boilers were
bubbling! The engines were back
to full speed.

They all thanked Percy for his help.

"Thank you, Percy!" they all whistled.

"See you at the funfair," peeped
Thomas, cheerfully.

It was getting late when Percy
finished his last delivery of coal.

He arrived at the funfair just as the
fireworks began.

The rockets soared high into the sky and the Chinese Dragon danced. All the children were delighted.

"The Fat Controller was right," tooted Percy. "Delivering coal is a very important job."